A
Swinging
Couple

Rachel Richards

This Edition: October 2015
eBook ISBN: 978-1-927679–38-8
Paperback ISBN: 978-1-927679-37-1

Contents

A Swinging Couple

Part One:

Full

Swing

Chapter One:

The Perfect Couple Again

Daniel held Vera's legs spread as he rammed his cock in and out of the shapely blonde while she licked Kelly's pussy who was squatting over her. Kelly balanced herself by holding onto and sucking Viktor's long thick cock. It was quite the show as all four of them moved in sync. None of them wanted this to end as the pace slowed down so that they could enjoy each thrust, lick or suck.

This was Kelly and Daniel's second session with Viktor and Vera and even though they didn't think it was possible, it was hotter than the first time that they all had gotten naked together. Kelly certainly thought so and squinted as Vera's tongue pleasured her. It was becoming too intense and she hung onto Viktor's cock for support. The orgasm that was building inside of her was so overpowering that she could barely concentrate on sucking the cock that was in her hands. She looked up at Viktor and her eyes filled with lust at the sight of him. She loved his strong features and the way that he looked at her. She bucked wildly as she came and Vera did her best to hang on to Kelly's tiny ass to keep her tongue on Kelly's clit. She did for a moment before Kelly collapsed beside Vera and moaned, "Oh that was so good."

Viktor put on a condom and moved between her legs. As Daniel rode Vera, Viktor slid his cock into Kelly who was still experiencing the highs of her climax. The feeling of her pussy being stuffed, emptied and stuffed again was overpowering. The pleasure was almost too much for her to handle.

"Oh god," she moaned. She looked up at the tall Russian man and studied his body as he rode her. He was lean, but his muscles were well toned. He was in shape and could move his body. In particular, his cock, and she treasured every one of his penetrations. "Fuck that feels good!"

"Fucking for pleasure," Daniel said. "What a concept." He laughed as everyone else continued to moan.

He looked at Kelly who had all four of her limbs wrapped around Viktor. Her eyes were closed, her mouth agape and she was moaning a lot. Daniel was a little jealous of how much she was enjoying being fucked by another man.

Kelly was oblivious to anything but the man and his cock that was penetrating her. She treasured each stroke and felt another orgasm build. Every move he made excited her and he was touching her in all of the right places.

Vera was enjoying herself too. She couldn't keep her eyes off Daniel and rose her head a few times to watch his cock disappear in and out of her pussy. She felt Kelly's hands on one of her tits and looked over to see her smiling at her. She smiled back and then told Daniel to stop and pull out. He did. She got up and while on all fours repositioned herself so that she could kiss Kelly. Daniel slid his cock into her and watched her make out with his girlfriend. The kiss was long and passionate as both women were on the verge of orgasm. The sight of it brought Daniel close to cumming as well.

Viktor shifted positions so that he could kiss Kelly's neck and this got a reaction from her. With his dick racing in and out of her, pleasuring her pussy, Vera's lips and tongue pleasuring her lips and now Viktor's tongue licking her behind her ear, drove her insane. Her pants became stronger and more frequent and this only encouraged her tormentors.

Dear fucking god, Kelly thought as another orgasm was about to burst.

Watching this, Daniel increased his pace and Vera

started to moan loudly.

"Okay on the count of three," Viktor said, "everyone cum."

"One," Daniel said.

"Two…"

"Three…"

Sperm flew out of both Daniel's and Viktor's cocks and into the condoms as Kelly arched her back and Vera jerked. Both women had an orgasm. All four of them came at the same time.

Daniel fell of to the side while Viktor to the right. Vera cuddled into Kelly and then Daniel spooned Vera. Viktor lay on his side and watched Kelly try to catch her breath. No one spoke for a few minutes.

"Incredible," Kelly said.

"Yes," Viktor added. "We're good together."

Great together, Kelly thought.

She watched the shadows on her bedroom ceiling and for the first time since they had all piled into the bedroom, she heard the noise of the traffic outside. It was late on a Saturday and she and Daniel had gotten laid big time.

Everyone that I want to fuck is naked on this bed, she thought. I hope that we all remain bed buddies forever.

She smiled at that pleasant thought.

The next day, the petite redhead sat on the couch and stared out the window wearing only an AC/DC concert t-shirt and pink panties. Her boyfriend was in the shower and for a moment she thought about going in and sucking his cock.

I just had it in me, Kelly thought. And I want it again? No. I want Viktor's cock.

She licked her lips and thought about what happened last night. It was really hot, she thought. He was perfect.

She closed her eyes and remembered being flat on her back with Viktor's cock inside of her. She looked forward to seeing them again in a few weeks. She couldn't wait to have dick inside of her again. However, it was maybe good that she did have to wait. Her pussy was sore from all the pounding it took last night and this morning. Remembering all that action made her wet.

"Fuck I love swinging," she whispered. "One lover is never enough."

She quietly went into the bathroom and pulled back the shower curtain. She surprised Daniel who was jerking off. "Oh my god," she said. "Again?"

"I was thinking of what we did last night and it made me hard." He continued to jerk himself.

She started to strip. "At least let me take care of that."

"Sure."

She got on her knees in the shower and took Daniel's cock into her mouth, pretending that it was Viktor's.

"I like watching you get off with other men," he said. "You love fucking them don't you?"

She knew that so she didn't bother answering him. And besides, her mouth was full.

"The way that you came last night... damn did you cum hard. I haven't seen you lose control like that in a long time."

True, she thought.

She sucked with more intensity as she felt him getting harder. She could tell that he was getting close to exploding.

"His big cock filled you tight little pussy...you were squirming with pleasure...back and forth...in

Rachel Richards

and out...Vera's pussy was squeezing my cock... harder and harder..."

She felt warm salty fluid in her mouth and after a few good jerks, he stopped. She knew that he was done. Well, for now, she thought. He will be back soon. The man is a sex machine. She looked at him and decided to change that to: a sexy machine.

A Swinging Couple

Chapter Two:
Back to the Club

Kelly was drunk with lust and the large amount of alcohol inside her helped to lessen her inhibitions. Swinging or wife swapping was such an unnatural thing to do in our anal society that even those who are highly sexed still have some doubts about what they are doing. Alcohol temporary erased all of those doubts in Kelly. It made her forget about the future and concentrate on the here and now.

She had looked forward to seeing Viktor and Vera again and couldn't wait to get naked with them. Daniel was excited too and why not? Their favourite couple was coming over and they were hoping to reproduce the last session. They were due to arrive at eight and if the first two sessions with them were any indication of things to come then this time should be torrid and this time Kelly would have at least three orgasms. She felt that the first one was already building.

In preparation, she wore a mini skirt and a blouse that barely covered her tits. It was very revealing and it wasn't meant for going out in public. It was for Viktor and Vera when they showed up. Well, it was mostly meant for Viktor when he got his hot body over to their place.

"Where are your panties?" Daniel said. "I can see everything when you bend over."

"Are you complaining?"

"Nope."

"I hope that Viktor likes."

"Oh he will. Oh lord will he like what he can see, which is everything."

Kelly flashed him a mischievous look.

"Oh you're bad."

"Just wait until you see how bad I am going to get tonight."

"Oh." Daniel was getting hard.

The phone rang. Kelly saw the number on the call display and was excited. "Hello friends," she said.

"Hi Kelly," Vera's voice said. She sounded down, which Kelly picked up on immediately.

"How are you doing?" She asked.

"Not good. Viktor and I decided to go our separate ways. We had a long talk today and we both agreed that it was for the best."

"Ah, why?" Kelly was upset.

"A few things, but it has mostly to do with the fact that Viktor has accepted a job in Alaska. There is good money for him there."

"And no work here. Damn!"

"No."

When Daniel saw the look on Kelly's face he knew that something was upsetting her.

"Do you need to talk?" She asked Vera.

"Thank you. I am okay. We knew that this was coming."

"Why don't you come over?"

"Ah no, I don't think that is a good idea."

"Do you want us...or me to come over?"

"Thank you, but I don't think that I would be very good company."

"I know. I would come over to help you through this."

"Thanks again, but I am okay. I knew that this was coming sooner or later. It just came a little sooner than I expected. I guess that is for the best."

"Okay." Kelly didn't sound convinced.

"I will call you soon. Okay?"

"Okay."

"Bye."

"Bye."

She hung up the phone and told her boyfriend what Vera told her. Their favorite fuck buddies were no longer together.

"Well, back to the club," Daniel said. He sighed. He was clearly disappointed.

"I guess." She sounded even more disappointed than he did.

"Hey. Who knows who else is out there? Maybe we will meet a couple that is even better than our Russian friends."

"Maybe, but I highly doubt that."

"I'm sure that we will in time."

"Maybe tonight?"

"I doubt it."

"Let's go and find out."

"Naw." She was down.

"She what else are we going to do, sit around here feeling sorry for ourselves? Let's go to the club and have some fun."

"I guess. But I am not wearing this."

She went through the motions of getting ready and Daniel came in a few times to hurry her up. "Just put on a pair of tight black pants and a blouse."

"I guess."

After dancing and drinking for an hour at the club, Kelly and Daniel were discouraged. They had walked in disheartened and so far they had failed to connect with anyone, not that there was anyone there who they wanted to connect with.

"I think that Vera and Viktor spoiled us," Daniel said.

"I think so too, but I am not lowering my standards."

"I don't blame you."

"Maybe we should go home and try next week."

He motioned to move, but she stood still. "Okay, we will stay for a bit longer."

"Yes."

Kelly's eyes caught something. It was a tall man with short blonde hair and no shirt on. It was the six pack that had gotten her attention. In her opinion he was lean with just the right amount of muscles. "Nice," she said. "Can you see what just walked in?"

"Actually, they have been here for awhile. The problem is that she is not much to look at. She's attractive, but not really my type. However I can see that you like him."

"Too bad. Don't want to take one for the team?"

He shrugged. "Let's dance."

The first song on the dance floor was uneventful and they just kept to themselves. For the next song German couple came onto the dance floor and Kelly kept glancing over at the tall blonde guy. He picked up on her signals and they danced their way closer. With his back turned to Kelly, the guy reach behind him to grab Kelly's ass.

Daniel saw this. "Those aren't my hands," he told her.

She glanced over her shoulder and saw that the German guy was facing away from her and had his large hands behind him to feel her ass. As he examined her beautiful little behind, she extended her hands to caress his forearms. She looked at Daniel. "Hot."

Daniel whispered, "Okay, one for the team."

Kelly smiled and bit her lip. "Thanks."

She turned around and let her hands caress his strong body. He liked the attention and turned around so she could admire the front. She rubbed her hands along his solid arms and chest. "Hello handsome," she said.

"Hello," he said with a strong accent.

His hands were on her perfectly shaped ass. He said something in German and Kelly saw a nice bulge in his black leather pants. She turned around and rubbed her ass against the bulge. She closed her eyes and let him touch her anywhere and everywhere he wanted to. She whimpered when he rubbed her crotch. If she wasn't wet before, she was now.

She turned around and looked up at him. He took the invite and leaned down to kiss her. Their lips met and he put his hands on her ass again.

Meanwhile Daniel and the German lady were dancing. She too had backed into him and he took that as an invite to explore her body. Her tits were bigger than he thought they looked and he enjoyed touching them. Still, she didn't do much for him. However, he did get an erection from watching Kelly get all hot and bothered. This, the woman who he was dancing with took as a sign that he was into her so she turned around and kissed him. He kissed her back and it wasn't bad.

The German guy started to undo Kelly's blouse, but she stopped him by putting her hands onto his and saying, "No." He tried again and she pulled away. "Sorry, no," she said. She didn't want her breasts exposed in public, but he took it the wrong way. He grabbed his wife's hands and said something in German that didn't sound too pleasant. Kelly and Daniel watched in disbelief as the couple walked away.

"That was weird," Daniel said.

"I think that he got pissed off because I wouldn't let him take my top off. I don't want to be nude on the dance floor."

"Me neither.'

"He took it the wrong way."

"Oh well. "Let's go home and fuck."

"I'm ready."

"You always are."

Daniel pulled out and after giving his cock a couple of good jerks, he started coming over Kelly. Each stroke after that brought another blob of semen that landed on her flat stomach. This surprised her as she watched his semen land. One blob landed on her chin and gasped.

"Oh, nice shot," she said.

A few more jerks and one big squirt later, he was done. He lay down beside Kelly.

"Was that good?" She asked.

"Yes. I love having sex with you."

"Me too. I mean love having sex with you too."

"And other people," he said playfully.

"Sometimes."

"But you're my favorite. Always."

"So, it is good that we sometimes strike out at the club. When we do, we come home and have great sex."

"Yes. That is not a bad second choice."

"Oh, I am not first choice?"

He rolled his eyes and didn't want to get into woman's insecurities. "Of course you are. At home. At the club, you are not even on the menu. I am there to fuck other women and watch you fuck other men and women. You are there to fuck other men and women. Otherwise, we just stay at home and fuck."

She clearly didn't like what he said. "Maybe we should take a break from the club."

"Sure you want to. How long?"

"A few weeks at least."

"Okay." He tried not to let his disappointment show.

"Are you sure?"

"Well, if you're not into it, then why do it. Let me know when you want to go again."

"I will."

He rolled over to go to sleep. He was angry for several reasons. One was that he was willing to take one for the team and she seemed to have forgotten that. The other reasons had to deal with the conversation that they just had and that in the mood that she was in there was no reasoning with her. "We will talk tomorrow," he said. "Goodnight."

"Goodnight." She was upset and got up. On the couch, the more that she thought about it, the more she knew that what he said wasn't wrong and that was it was her that was being unreasonable. He only said the truth about his intentions and she knew that from the start.

So what is the problem, she thought. I have a great guy loves me and won't fuck another woman without permission. But he should only want to fuck me. I should be the center of his attention.

Her thoughts drifted to Viktor and how much she missed fucking him. I hope that I can find another guy like him, she thought then realized the double standard. So, I can play and Daniel can't...that isn't fair. In that case, we both stop then.

She sighed and realized that she didn't want to stop swinging and in fact, she wanted to do more. She wanted a bunch of men like Viktor and that meant that it wasn't fair of Daniel for wanting the same thing.

We both want to fuck good looking strangers and then come home to each other, she thought.

Again another wave of emotion told her that her man should want only her and no one else and who cares if she wanted to step out on him.

Sometimes I hate being a woman, she thought. I wish that I was a man so I could want to fuck everything in sight without feeling guilty about it. Men are born sluts and women have too many feelings that make us feel guilty and insecure.

After a big sigh she decided that she was going to be more in touch with her masculine side. Flashes of both beautiful naked men and women raced through her mind and she wanted them all. She wanted to rub her tits and pussy against all of their hot bodies and never stop.

Feeling emotionally more stable, she went back to bed and cuddled into Daniel. "Let's try the club again next week," she said.

"Sure." He rolled over and put his arm around her.

"I understand why you want to fuck other woman."

"You do?"

"Yes. I want us to fuck every hot person out there. Let's go wild."

Chapter Three:
In Search of Hot Bodies

Kelly was excited all week and couldn't wait for Saturday night. She wore her white dress that showed the majority of what cleavage she had and most of her legs and ass. It was important for her to look her best because she wanted to attract every hot man she could. She was on the market.

Daniel checked her out and felt movement in his pants. He admired her thin legs, her round little ass... "What?" She asked him when she caught him starting at her.

"You look great," she said then adjusted his penis.

"Do I?"

"Hell yeah. You're making me hard."

Kelly felt sexy and walked into the club with confidence. On the way to the bar they were intercepted by a couple that they had chatted to a few times. According to Daniel she was do-able, but there was no way that Kelly could get it on with him. Unfortunately, they either didn't get the message that they weren't into them or they just didn't take no for an answer.

After a few minutes, Daniel excused himself to get

Kelly a drink, leaving Kelly to listen to Julie and Bert talk about how good their trip to Hedonism was. Kelly was more interested in the actual resort than all the swinging that went on there.

"How was the food?" she asked.

"Good in some of the restaurants," Julie said.

Bert said, "You should go. We are going back in a few months. Join us."

When Daniel came back he saw that another couple had joined them. He had never seen them before. It was apparent that they all knew each other.

The woman had blonde curly hair and was maybe a touch overweight. She was attractive and the way she looked at Daniel told everyone that she was attracted to him. He handed a beer to Kelly and stood beside her. "Daniel," he said to her.

"Sara," she said brightly.

"I'm Earl," the guy said. He was attractive in Kelly's eyes. Not gorgeous, but the more that she spoke to him the better looking he became.

"Well," Sara said. "You two talk and let us know."

"Okay."

Daniel was confused and after Earl and Sara left he

looked at Kelly.

"So what do you think of Earl and Sara?" She asked him.

"Sure. She should be fun to play with." He shrugged. "You? What do you think of him?"

"Fine. I could do him."

"Why do you ask?"

"Because Sara just asked me if we want to go into the back with them. I am game."

"Why not?" He saw them on the dance floor. "Let's join them."

"No, not yet."

"Why?"

"They'll be back in a minute and I want to finish my drink."

When Earl and Sara came back to the table Kelly smiled at them.

"Shall we go to the back?" Sara said. She grabbed Earl's hand and walked towards the back. Kelly and Daniel followed.

The four of the strip and put their clothes into the lockers. Sara was the last to put her towel on and when she was ready they wandered around the back looking for an empty bed. Most beds were occupied with two or more people pleasuring each other. A steady stream of moans was heard.

Kelly always thought that this part was surreal. All of those naked bodies grinding together, she thought. This was an orgy and I am about to be part of the fun.

They found an empty bed and Sara dropped her towel and lay down on the bed. Earl jumped on top of her blocking Daniel's attempts to kiss Sara. Since Earl was in the way he kissed his girlfriend instead.

They want to do it this way, Kelly thought. Ease into it by playing with familiar territory first. Okay.

She kissed Daniel and that was good. It was always good with him.

They looked over and Earl was making his way down Sara's body. He fondled and kissed her big tits then went down between her legs.

Daniel leaned over and cupped one of Sara's breasts while he kissed the other one. Kelly waited for Earl to come to her. Instead Earl kept looking at Daniel kiss and play with his wife. He was clearly uncomfortable with this. Daniel didn't pick up on that and said to him, "Why don't you play with Kelly while I explore your hot wife."

Julie was by the curtain and asked, "Can we join in." Bert was standing behind her.

Kelly knew that she should of closed those curtains.

Before her or Daniel could say no, Sara blurted, "Sure. The more the better."

Julie went straight for Daniel's cock and started sucking. Bert motioned to get between Kelly's legs. He spread her legs and had his head between her legs before she could protest.

Earl froze and glared at Julie and Daniel. Kelly knew that this wasn't happening and she wasn't surprised that he jumped up and grabbed his towel before he left.

Daniel didn't notice but Sara did. She got up. "Sorry, be right back," she said.

"Um…" Daniel was surprised.

"Just hang on," Kelly whispered to him. "Someone is not ready."

"Who? Sara. No, she is ready to go."

"Not her. Him."

"Oh. I thought that they were experienced swingers."

"Nope. This is their first time."

"Really?"

Sara came back and said, "Sorry guys. We have to go. It isn't you."

"Don't worry about it," She said to her. "We understand."

This left Kelly and Daniel with two people that they didn't want to swing with and they didn't have the heart to say no. Kelly closed her eyes and tried to enjoy Bert's pussy eating technique. He wasn't bad, but didn't look forward to fucking him. She looked over at Daniel. He had Julie down on all fours and was riding her hard.

She does have a nice little body, she thought. Nice ass. Daniel will like that.

They locked eyes and Daniel rolled his eyes. Kelly suppressed a laugh and rolled her eyes too. She watched her man fuck another woman and loved the way he moved. He was in good shape, strong and handsome. She was basically masturbating over him, but instead of playing with herself, Bert was doing that for her. He ate while she lusted after Daniel.

She had a little orgasm, but pretended that it was bigger than it was. Bert was pleased with himself and got up. He slipped on a condom and was about to enter her when she told him to hang on. She went down on all fours, facing Daniel who now had Julie on her back. This was better to look at than tired old Bert. Bert entered and Kelly motioned for Daniel to kiss her. He did.

Julie reached up and felt Kelly's tits. Then she moved over to get underneath them. She took one of them into her mouth. Kelly was enjoying this when she didn't remember who was the owner of the cock that was inside of her. When she remembered it was a turn off.

Kelly kept in that position until Bert came then she waited until Daniel came before she excused herself to go to the washroom. When she got back, the other couple was gone.

"They had other people to fuck," Daniel said wryly.

Quietly she said, "From now on the curtains stay closed so that doesn't happen again."

"Well, Julie does have a nice body."

Kelly glared at him. "Don't even entertain it."

"Sorry."

I guess that I just took one for the team, she

thought. But then again, Daniel really didn't want me to. Ugh. God, why can't all swingers be hot?

She didn't want to think that she just got fucked by someone like Bert.

Daniel phoned around six on Thursday and Kelly knew what was going on before she even picked up the phone. "Hey," she said. "You are still at work?"

"Yep and I am not leaving for a while. Deadlines."

"And dinner? Do you want me to save you something to heat up?"

"No, we've sent out Billy out for it. It is on the company."

"Okay, so when should I expect you?"

"Before ten I hope, but don't wait up."

"That doesn't sound good."

"Nope."

"Are you fucking another woman?" She joked.

He laughed. "I wish!"

She smiled. She knew that if he was he would tell her.

Or would he, she thought? No, he would tell me if he wanted something, he always does. That is our deal. So stop worrying about if he is fooling around on me or not. He is working. Poor guy, he sounds exhausted. And I am bored.

She decided to continue to read the novel that she had started a few days ago. It was an erotic novel about a group of people who got together once a year to fuck each other. That is where she thought that the novel should stop, but the author decided to put in a lot of drama with jealous boyfriends and girlfriends and insecurities. That part was okay, but she just wanted the sex. Just like now. She didn't want all of that crap, just hot fucking.

Now, she thought. If I was a writer what would I do? Hmmm…

Let's start with a nice resort in the Caribbean and a number of couples. Three? No, four. Of course there is Daniel and myself, so that means we need a blonde and brunette. Let's give them both big tits and the fourth woman can be another redhead. The men can be tall, lean and handsome. I want one of them to be a bodybuilder. The other two must also be in good shape. Short haired and handsome.

Without a thought she undid her pants and slipped a hand into her panties. Masturbation was automatic these days and her only fear was that she might do it in public one of these days.

"Thank you for going with me last night to the orgy," Daniel said.

"No problem. I really enjoyed it," Kelly said brightly. "And those bodies intertwined in passion, touching, sucking, fucking..." She stopped, sighed then added, "God, I am such a slut!"

He laughed. "That is what I love about you." He put his arm around her, looked down at her cleavage and added, "At one point you were riding some guy who had some woman sitting on his face and taking turns sucking me and another guy. You looked pretty into it."

"I was. I had a big cock inside of me and don't know how many hands were on my body."

Kelly arched her back and came at the thought of a room full of hot bodies around her.

After she came back to reality, she thought that her little fantasy was pretty silly. However, it did the job. It made her cum. Now, she wanted men to line up and apply for the job of making her cum.

She smiled. She knew that Daniel liked having that job.

Chapter Four:
Coming On Strong

The woman had the air of being very prim and proper and the last thing she would do is have sex with anyone including her husband. She made June Cleaver look like a slut in comparison.

Kelly saw her come into the club and said to Daniel, "Okay someone just doesn't belong here."

"Like a fish out of water," he said.

She looked at the woman's husband who appeared to be normal. "I bet you that this was all his idea and that she really doesn't want to be here."

"She is pretty though."

Kelly nodded. "Yes she is."

"Let's dance."

"Sure."

A few songs later, Kelly was surprised when the prude and her man came onto the dance floor. She was surprised even more when she saw that she allowed him to grab her ass through her long skirt.

"Somewhere amongst all that fabric is a nice ass," Daniel joked. "Somewhere."

Kelly laughed. "I will die if she takes off her jacket to get down to only two layers of clothing."

Daniel raised an eyebrow. "Are you sure that she isn't going braless?"

Kelly almost doubled over with laughter. When she stopped laughing she said, "Too funny."

The woman spun around and backed into her man. He cupped her breasts and she looked directly at Daniel. He watched the guy's hand travel down her body and she licked her lips.

"Maybe she is a sexpot after all," Daniel whispered to Kelly.

She turned and backed into Daniel to see what he was talking about. The women were now only a few feet away from each other. The woman locked eyes and since Kelly thought that the tall thin blonde was attractive she moved forward and pressed herself against her. Their boobs rubbed together and Kelly studied the other woman.

She seems comfortable with this, Kelly thought.

She felt a hand on her ass and it was the woman's. This removed any doubt so Kelly returned the favor and put her hands on the loose shirt that contained an ass. She found it and it was smaller than hers. The guy moved away and motioned for

Rachel Richards

Daniel to take his spot. He did and the guy moved behind Kelly, who liked him pressing against her behind.

It was getting steamy and the woman seemed to like the attention of being pressed between Kelly and Daniel. She never protested Daniel's hands on her bum. Nor did she seem to mind when Daniel cupped her tits.

Without warning, she tensed up. Kelly instinctively backed off, allowing the woman to walk away. That she did. She walked off the dance floor and her man followed. Daniel watched the woman walk right out of the club while Kelly shook her head.

"What happened?" Daniel said.

"We came on too strong and she got scared."

"Yes, we did, but we were fooled. We thought that she was ready."

"Apparently she wasn't. Our original assessment was correct. She isn't a swinger."

"Well, not yet. It may take a long time, but maybe one day."

"A long long time."

"Next…" Daniel said.

"No, drink first."

At the bar, Kelly laid eyes on an older woman that she had never seen before and was stunned. She was both jealous and attracted to her. The woman was blonde with high cheek bones and green eyes and was very pretty. But it was her figure that Kelly was overwhelmed with. She had long legs, nice hips and large breasts on a thin figure.

The woman noticed that Kelly was gawking at her and came over. "Hello," she said. "I am Gina."

"Kelly."

"Daniel."

A man came behind Gina and she said that this is my husband, "Albert."

Kelly thought that Albert was good looking, but it was Gina that she was enthralled with. The woman could do anything that she wanted to do to her. If the woman spotted it then she kept it to herself. It had been a long time since Daniel saw Kelly so taken with another woman and that turned him on.

As the women spoke, the men listened. The focus was clearly on Gina and she knew it. Finally Gina said, "Let's dance." It wasn't a question. It was an order that Kelly gladly followed.

The women walked onto the dance floor while the men stopped at a table at the edge.

Gina put her arms around the petite redhead and pulled her close. It didn't take long for Gina to put her lips against Kelly's who kissed her back with passion.

"Oh that was nice," Kelly said.

"It was." Gina ran her hand through Kelly's hair. "Are you a natural redhead?"

"Yes I am."

"Oh nice. I would love to go down on you."

Kelly giggled. "Oh my."

"So I take it that is a yes?"

Kelly nodded and licked her lips. She glared into Gina's eyes.

Gina took Kelly's hand and said, "Come." They headed towards the back. Their men followed.

Instead of going into the play area, Gina stopped at a couch in the back corner. "Here. Sit," she said.

Kelly sat on the couch and stared up at Gina. Gina knelt in front of Kelly, put her hands on her legs and then leaned in for a kiss. Kelly put her arms around her and pressed her lips against the other woman's soft lips.

Gina's hands slowly slid Kelly's dress up to expose her panties. The men by now had taken a seat and were watching the action from the side. As the women were still kissing, Gina took hold of the sides of the panties and Kelly raised her butt so that they could slide off. Kelly sat back down and raised her legs so Gina could pull them off completely. Gina tossed them behind her onto the floor. Albert picked them up and smelled them.

Gina broke off the kiss and Kelly sat back, watching Gina put a hand on each knee to slowly spread her legs. She moaned with each kiss to her legs and wished that Gina would hurry up. "Eat me," she said.

"In time," Gina said playfully.

"I am so wet for you."

"I know."

Gina's lips landed on Kelly's pussy lips and that excited all four of them. The men were both hard as they were enjoying the show. Gina's fingers spread Kelly's lips to let her tongue have better access. Kelly moaned and put her hands on top of Gina's head.

At that moment in Kelly's world, there was

nothing else but Gina and the wonderful orgasm that was building inside of her, thanks to Gina's tongue.

"This won't take long," Daniel whispered to Albert. "She is going to pop."

Albert smiled. "I think that I am as well."

Another couple stopped to watch Kelly get off. Her back was starting to arch and she was sinking further into the couch. She put her hands over head and rocked her hips. Gina continued to lick and drive Kelly crazy.

Kelly briefly opened her eyes to see four people watching her and Gina. Two of them she didn't know. She didn't care she was well on her way to having the orgasm of her life. Well, at least a very good one.

A finger slid into her pussy and went right for her g-spot.

Oh Jesus, Kelly thought. I am not going to last.

She didn't. With Gina's tongue working her clit and her finger massaging her g-spot, Kelly had no choice but to arch her back and cum. This she did violently. She bucked and moaned loudly.

"Very nice," Daniel said.

Gina stood up, wiped her mouth and then took her drink from her husband. Daniel retrieved her panties from Albert and helped her put them back on. "Thank you," Kelly said.

"You good?"

"I am great." She smiled and sighed.

"Content?"

"Very."

To Daniel's disappointment Gina and Albert informed them that they were about to leave. "So soon?" He asked.

"Are you going to eat and run?" Kelly mumbled, but no one other than Albert heard. He laughed.

Gina grabbed Daniel's arm and told him, "We have my daughter coming for lunch tomorrow so we don't want to stay up too late. We will come again next week."

They exchanged numbers and the next week, Kelly and Daniel went to the club, expecting to meet them there. They stood at a table by the dance floor.

"I want to go all the way with them," Daniel said to Kelly.

"That would be fine. What she did to me last week

would really hot." She smiled.

"It was really hot, but nothing for me."

"Maybe Albert could blow you?" She laughed.

"Funny. I don't think that I am his type. And besides, he isn't my type."

"Well, Gina is mine."

"Gina is everyone's type."

They came in and after a few drinks and laughs later, the woman hit the dance floor. This gave Daniel the opportunity to ask Albert. "So, besides Gina being into women, what are you guys into?"

"Not much else. Gina gets to play with women and I get to watch."

"So, you have never swapped then?"

"Hell no."

"So what is in it for you?"

"I get to watch my beautiful wife lusting after another woman. Then we go home and have great sex."

What came next was basically a carbon copy of what happened last week. It was hot, but Daniel wanted more than just watching. Later, on the way home Kelly said, "I am getting a little frustrated by the girl only stuff."

"Me too," Daniel said strongly. He told her what Albert told him about their restrictions. "Time to move on."

"I think so."

Daniel sighed. "We are in a rut."

"I guess." She looked at him. "What is it?"

"I want to take a break from the club."

"Why? Because I am getting action and you aren't."

"Um...yeah, that and it was great the first time and fine the second, but...it is more that we can't meet anyone...and the fact that this is costing me money. I don't want to pay just to be a spectator. I can rent a porno for much cheaper."

Kelly had mixed feelings about this. She really liked Gina, but she could understand Daniel's frustrations. He was a man of action. He wasn't a watcher.

Reluctantly she said, "Okay. We can take a short break." She wanted to get deeper into the lifestyle, not pull back. This wasn't good and wouldn't work if her man wasn't on board.

He saw her disappointment and said, "If you want

to meet Gina on the side then fine."

"No, I don't want to do that. Getting some on the side is not what we are doing here. If we play we play together, right?"

"Yes. That is the deal."

"You're not fooling around on the side are you?"

The way that he looked at her, told her that he wasn't. "No. Why did you even ask that?"

"You have been working a lot lately."

"Yes, I have been **working**." He was a little upset.

"Sorry, I don't know why I asked that."

"Because that is what you have been thinking that's why."

She didn't answer because she knew that he was right. "Sorry."

"After all of this and the promises that we made, you are still worried that I am fucking someone on the side." He groaned.

"I am sorry. I guess that I am a little upset about you not being satisfied."

"Are you?"

"Yes."

He stopped and said, "Then do something about it." He pulled her down an alley and leaned against a wall. "Blow me."

"Here?"

"Why not?"

"Okay."

She squatted and unzipped his pants. He was hard and she watered her mouth. Time to keep my man happy, she thought as she took his cock into her mouth.

Chapter Five:

Vacation

A month later, Kelly and Daniel flew to Cancun for a much needed week in the sun. They got to the resort in the afternoon and were pretty much satisfied with their ocean view room. It wasn't the most luxurious of suites but it was nice. After they unpacked they went to check out the place.

As they walking along the path that took them to the pool, Kelly was thinking of how much she would love if Viktor and Vera were here.

After dinner, they went to the beach bar to enjoy the ambience. It was a clear night with a light breeze and the sounds of the waves hitting the shore added to their mood.

"A Margaritas and beer," Daniel said.

"You should try something other than beer," Kelly told him.

"Why? I like beer."

"We're in the land of rum so you should have something with rum in it."

"Why? I am also in the land of Corona so…"

She groaned. "You are so boring sometimes."

"Really?" He laughed.

"You know what I mean."

As their drinks came, a middle aged couple came to the bar a couple of seats to Kelly's left and she marveled how dark they were. As she had just gotten here, she had yet to get any sun and was envious of their tans. She turned to Daniel and said, "I am getting some major sun tomorrow."

"Of course. That is why we are here."

"I want to get as dark as they are."

"Sure." Daniel spotted another couple who sat down at the bar to his left. They were African-American. "How about as dark as them?"

"Ah, no." Kelly laughed.

"Hi, how are you?" The guy said to them.

"Good and you."

They introduced themselves as Mark and Katrina from Philadelphia and this was their second last night before they had to fly home. Kelly was attracted to them both immediately. He had a good built, curly black hair and his beard was kept short. She was curvy and pretty. Kelly loved her long black hair and her warm smile.

"Two Sex on the Beach," Mark said to the

bartender. "Want one?" He said to Kelly.

"Sure, I'll have one too," Kelly added.

All three of them looked at Daniel. "Oh sure why not. I'll try one too."

Mark turned to the bartender and said, "That will be four for Sex on the Beach."

Katrina laughed and rolled her eyes. She looked at Kelly and said, "I apologize for my husband. He thinks that he is being so funny."

"Don't worry about it," Kelly said. "Just wait until mine gets going."

"Great. Now we have two of them."

A few rounds later, Mark was ordering more drinks and Katrina went to the washroom.

"I think that they are swingers," Kelly whispered to Daniel.

"I think that you want them to be," Daniel joked.

She smiled. "Yes I do." She licked her lips and stared at Daniel.

"Let's see how this unfolds."

"Sure."

Mark placed the drinks in front of Kelly and Daniel

and as they waited for Katrina to come back from the washroom said, "I got an idea. Let's take our drinks down to the beach."

"Sex on the Beach on the beach," Daniel said. "Why not?"

The four of them wandered down from the beach bar to where there wasn't anyone else. The moonlight became the only source of light. The woman walked together with the men trailing behind.

"So Kelly," Mark said. "When you have chicken do you order the dark or white meat?"

"Oh god Mark," Katrina said. She was laughing.

Kelly stopped and turned around to face the men. "White most of the time, but once in a while I have the dark meat." She smiled at Mark and licked her lips.

"Oh," Mark said. "Good answer."

Not to be outdone, Katrina said, "I actually prefer white meat." She looked at Daniel.

"Oh girl," Mark said, "Don't be cruel. I hope that you're joking."

"I'm not," Daniel said.

The four of them stood there laughing as they

faced each other. Kelly would not object if Mark tried to kiss her right then and there. In fact, she wanted him to and judging by Katrina's body language she wanted Daniel.

Mark held up his drink. "After we're done these, do you guys want to help us raid our mini-bar?" Mark asked.

"Sounds like a plan," Daniel said. He looked at the girls who both nodded.

Their suite was a little nicer than Kelly and Daniel's and as they got in Katrina grabbed Kelly's hand and said, "Come. I have to show you this. You won't believe the size of the bathroom."

The men went towards the bar and Mark asked, "What do you think that Kelly wants to drink?"

"Anything."

"How about rum and cola's all around?"

"Sure. She is easy."

Mark smiled. "She seems to like to have fun."

"Oh yeah. She's a party girl."

"Cool. Katrina can get pretty wild herself."

"Yeah. How wild?"

Daniel looked into Mark's eyes. "Wilder than

49

Kelly."

"I am not sure about that."

"Oh yeah, if I told her to suck your cock, Katrina would without hesitation."

"And Kelly would suck yours."

Mark was a little shocked. "Really?"

"Yes. I've seen her do it before."

"Well, I've seen Katrina with two guys at once and I wasn't one of them."

"Really? What were you doing?"

"I was with the guy's wives at the time."

"An orgy. Cool."

"Yes. Are you guys up for a mini-orgy?"

"Yes."

Meanwhile the women were in the huge bathroom and Kelly couldn't believe how big it was. They were still holding hands.

"I've been in smaller hotel rooms that this," Kelly said looking around.

"Look at the shower. It could hold at least eight people."

"That it could. Too bad we didn't have four more

people."

Katrina smiled. "Yes, too bad." She spun and faced Kelly. "You guys are fun."

"Well, we like to have fun."

"How much fun?" Her tone was serious and she looked right at Kelly.

"As much fun as we can have."

"Nice. How about sex?"

"Like I said, as much fun as we can have."

"Does that include swinging?"

"Yes."

"Hard swaps?"

"Yes."

"Would you guys like to swing with us?"

Kelly leaned in and put her lips against Katrina's. They were both locked in a passionate kiss when Mark walked in. Daniel was behind him. "You ladies, we have a king size bed in the other room that you can use."

Katrina pulled Kelly past the men and led her to the bed where she pushed her onto it. Kelly landed on her back with her legs spread. She didn't bother to close them. Katrina slipped off her sundress and let it fall to the floor. Then she positioned herself between Kelly's legs and lay on top of her.

After a long passionate kiss, Mark tapped Katrina on the shoulder and told her, "My turn."

She got up, walked over to Daniel and kissed him. His hands reached down to feel her ass. Mark's pants were already off when he got between Kelly's legs. She wrapped all four limbs around him as they kissed.

Katrina dropped to her knees and tugged at Daniel's pants. He didn't mind. He watched Mark and Kelly make out as Katrina dropped his pants and underwear and take his erection into her mouth. Mark moved down Kelly's body and took off her panties. He lifted her dress and buried his head into her pussy. Kelly put her hands up and squirmed with passion.

"Nice," Daniel said. The feeling of her lips together with the sight of Kelly getting off brought a smile to his face. He was in paradise.

As Mark continued to eat her, Kelly raised herself and lifted her dress over her head. Then she undid her bra and tossed that at Daniel. She smiled at him and he gave her the thumbs up. She returned it then fell back, putting her hands on top of Mark's head and wrapping her legs around his broad shoulders.

"My turn," Katrina said as she got off her knees. She took off her bra and panties. She lay beside Kelly and spread her legs.

Daniel dropped to his knees and went straight for her pussy. Katrina leaned to her side and took one of Kelly's tits into her hands. Her tongue played with the nipple. If Kelly was close to orgasm before, she was on the verge of one now.

From between Katrina's legs, he heard the familiar sounds of Kelly having an orgasm and judging by the intensity of it, it was a good one. He continued to eat the woman and he looked up to see that Kelly had one of Katrina's oversized tits in her hand.

Mark reached into the night stand and pulled out a box of condoms. He got one out and placed the box on the table. "Are you ready for this," he said to Kelly.

Kelly looked over her shoulder and saw Mark's erection. He was a good size with two big balls.

"I do love dark meat," she said and got ready for him.

"Open wide." He slid his cock into Kelly. She

moaned, but was drowned out by Katrina who had reached climax.

"That's one for Katrina," Mark said.

Daniel reached behind Mark and grabbed a condom from the box on the night stand. He slipped it on as Mark's cock raced in and out of Kelly, much to her delight.

Daniel slipped into the dark skinned woman and as he rode her, watched how her tits jiggled.

Mark pulled out and said to Kelly, "Doggie."

Of course, she thought. All men want to look at my ass.

She didn't mind because being on all fours allowed her to play with Katrina's big tits. This she did as Mark shoved his cock back into her pussy. She concentrated on squeezing her lips together as tight as she could.

"Damn woman you have a great ass," he said.

Kelly's mouth was full of Katrina's tit so she didn't answer. Daniel looked over to see Mark's big cock disappear between Kelly's pussy lips and then pull out again. Kelly moaned with each thrust. Daniel then watched his own cock disappear into Katrina's pussy.

Kelly and Daniel held hands as they walked back to their suite.

"It seems that our luck is changing," Daniel said.

"It is about time."

"Was that true about you sometimes preferring dark meat?"

"No. I just thought it would add to the sexual tension."

He smiled. "That it did."

A Swinging Couple

Chapter Six:
The Right Time and
Place

The next Saturday after they got back, they were back at the club and both of them had enjoyed the break. Any tension or jealousy was gone after a month of working on their relationship. It didn't need much repair, just a little time. The vacation helped and screwing Mark and Katrina really helped. They felt like they were back on track.

They were relieved that Gina and her watcher husband weren't there. Unfortunately, the night started off the same way that things had been going for them before they met them. There was nothing there for them so they danced, talked to a few people they knew and drink. A couple of hours later, Daniel wanted to leave.

"One last dance," Kelly said.

"Okay."

On the floor, Daniel noticed a cute little brunette. She was wearing black shorts and a t-shirt that showed off her curves. Nice tits, he thought.

She noticed him checking her out and turned to

look at him. Daniel grabbed Kelly, spun her around so that she was facing the woman with nice tits. Kelly smiled when she saw the tall man that she was dancing with.

The woman moved towards Kelly and pressed against her. Her large tits rubbed against Kelly's boobs. "Well hello," Kelly said.

"Hi," she said. "Let's switch."

The girls spun in a half circle and the tall man moved behind Kelly. His hands were quickly on her. She looked up at him and smiled. He leaned down and kissed her. She kissed him back.

"That was quick," Daniel mumbled.

"Looks like fun," she said. She spun around to face him.

As they kissed Daniel thought, one minute you are alone with your wife and the next minute you are making out with a stranger.

A few steamy dances later, they introduced themselves as Glen and Lisa.

"Sorry," Glen said to Daniel. "I didn't mean to kiss Kelly so quickly. Halfway through I was wondering if I was allowed to do this."

"If you weren't I would of said something."

"And I wouldn't be kissing you," Kelly said.

"It is all good," Lisa said. "I would like a drink."

The guys left to get drinks for everyone, giving the women a chance to talk.

Lisa asked, "So, can I ask how experienced you two are?"

"Sure. We have done some things."

"Hard or soft swaps?"

"Oh hard. What is the point of only doing a soft swap? If you are going to step out with someone you might as well go all the way."

Lisa smiled. "Good. Us too. We don't see the point of just having foreplay with another couple. Fuck me or don't bother."

"How long have you been doing this?"

"About four years," she said and went on to list a number of things that they have done, including a number of orgies.

Kelly listened to all the things that they have done and got the impression that they were pretty hard core swingers. Where Kelly and Daniel dabbled, they went in with both feet. It seemed that they slept with a different couple every weekend. Kelly and Daniel would too, but they were fussier about who they got naked with.

When Daniel and Glen got back, he also heard about some of their exploits and was a little intimidated by it.

"So, you two are obviously comfortable with swapping, right?" Glen asked.

Kelly looked at Daniel and smiled. "Yep. We have had some fun."

"Great. Do you guys want to come back with us to our hotel?" Glen asked.

"Sure," Kelly said. She looked at Daniel who asked, "Where are you staying?"

"The Marriot," Glen said.

"Nice," Kelly said.

Lisa clapped her hands and was clearly excited. "Then it is all set. Let's go have some fun."

The four of them walked to the hotel and took the elevator to the sixth floor.

From the elevator, Glen took hold of Kelly's hand and the pair of them walked down the hallway together.

"That's nice," Daniel said to Glen.

"Sweet."

Glen opened the door and held it open for the ladies. They walked in and Kelly said, "Nice suite."

"Well, not quite, but it is still better than a normal hotel room," Lisa said.

Besides a king size bed there was a full size couch, an arm chair and a coffee table. Kelly said down on the couch and Lisa went into the bedroom. Glen asked, "Wine?"

"Please," Kelly said.

"Sure," Daniel added.

"I forgot to ask," Glen said. "Are you guys into hard swaps or soft swaps?" He looked right at Kelly.

Kelly shifted in her seat and licked her lips. "Hard swaps."

"Oh," Glen said and smiled. The two of them locked eyes and Daniel wondered why they didn't start fucking right then and there. Kelly thought so too. She was in heat and she left no doubt in Glen's mind as what she wanted him to do to her. Her eyes drifted down to his crotch and she wondered what his cock was like. I will find out soon, she thought.

Lisa came out of the washroom and sat beside

Kelly. She was about a foot away and it was clear that she wasn't really interested in girl on girl. She smiled at Daniel.

Glen sat down beside Kelly at the end of the couch. Daniel moved to the other end of the couch to sit beside Lisa.

"So how often do you guys come into the city?" Kelly asked Lisa.

"Depends on our schedules. Sometimes it is a couple of times a month. At others it can be a few months. It is hard with kids."

"I bet."

"How often do you guys go to the club?" Glen asked.

"About two or three times a month."

"You're lucky to live so close," Lisa said. "How many kids do you have?"

"None. We like being free."

"God, no kids is freedom." She looked at her husband. "What were we thinking?"

Glen laughed. "We could sell them? Could you imagine how much fucking we could do if we didn't have kids?"

"Not to us," Kelly said laughing. "We don't want kids." Her head was resting against the back of the couch and she was basically reclined.

No one spoke after that. The mood was filled with sexual tension. The four horny people on the couch were done with talking. Daniel leaned forward and Lisa rested against the back, looking at him. Glen leaned in and locked lips with Kelly. His hands travelled down her body and undid the button of her pants. Then he unzipped her pants. Meanwhile her left hand returned the favor. She undid his zipper and slid her small hand in to touch a large hard cock.

Oh my god, she thought. He is big. Very big.

He pulled up her blouse to reveal her tits and his mouth went to her exposed flesh. She took a nipple in his mouth and played with it.

She looked over and saw that Daniel had one of Lisa's nipples in his mouth. God, she has big tits, she thought.

Glen pulled Kelly up and walked her over to the bed. He helped her undress and let her sit down on the bed. As he undressed she moved to lay on her stomach, positioning her face only inches away from his crotch. There was a huge bulge in his underwear that she couldn't help but notice.

"All of it," she commanded.

He slid off his underwear and his cock pointed straight at Kelly. Without hesitation she reached out and pulled him closer. When he was at the edge of the bed, she engulfed his cock.

After a few minutes, he said, "Let me return the favor. Get onto your back."

By the time he finished the sentence, Kelly had turned around and was flat on her back, ready to be eaten.

His hands held her legs as he lowered his head towards her red haired pussy. His tongue made contact with her flesh and she squirmed. She was in heaven. A hot guy with a big dick was pleasing her and she was already on the verge of having an orgasm. His tongue touched her again and she moaned loudly.

Meanwhile, Daniel had momentarily stopped admiring Lisa's big tits and the two of them were undressing. As they were moving towards the bed, Daniel told her to assume the same position as Kelly and she gladly obeyed. Within seconds of laying on the bed, she too was moaning.

Kelly arched her back and came. That's one, she thought.

Glen lay on the bed with his oversized cock pointing straight up. His hands were busy unwrapping a condom. Kelly got between his legs and demonstrated how good of a cock sucker she was. He moaned and closed his eyes. This was good, he thought.

She took it all into her mouth and passionately sucked it.

Meanwhile, Daniel was getting sucked off by Lisa. It was good, but the sight of watching Kelly suck cock was better. Still, both women were highly attentive in their tasks and when Kelly stopped, Glen said, "Thank you."

"You're welcome."

Kelly waited until Glen slipped the condom on and then she slowly lowered herself onto him. His cock gently invaded her pussy, pushing her lips aside further than they had been pushed before. She shuttered. Another orgasm was building.

Lisa got onto her back and Daniel walked over to the dresser to get a condom. He slipped it on and when he got back, she was ready for him. He slid his rock hard cock easily into her.

This is a good fuck, Daniel thought as he enjoyed Lisa's body. God I love pussy!

He looked over and saw that Kelly's eyes were closed as she rode Glen's dick. Yep, she is having fun. She loved dick.

Kelly was lost in pleasure and the only thing that matter to her right now was how good Glen's cock felt rubbing against her pussy lips. Each stroke was better than the one before. She rode him steadily until she heard Glen ask if they could switch positions.

"Sure," she said. "Which one?"

"Doggie."

She got down on all fours and he put his hands on her waist. Slowly he slid his big cock into her. "What a great ass," he cried out. "Beautiful."

He humped her and never took his eyes off her butt. Kelly liked the pace he set with his big weapon. It wasn't too quick or slow.

Daniel had Lisa on her back and was admiring the way that her large tits rested against her. Glen had Kelly's perfect ass to look at and he had a pair of nice tits.

"Let me on top," Lisa said.

Daniel lay on his back and Lisa lowered herself onto his cock. She moaned as she started to hump him. He watched the way that her tits bounced and this made him harder.

"Great tits," he said.

She was too busy moaning to respond. Daniel reached up and grabbed both tits. Flesh spilled out of his hands and he thought of that old phrase, `Bigger than a handful is wasteful.' He disagreed and augmented the saying to say, `Bigger than a handful is wonderful!'

Meanwhile, Glen had increased the pace as he still held Kelly's ass. He mumbled, "Beautiful ass, beautiful ass…"

He groaned and clinched his eyes and everyone in the room new that he was cumming. He finished and slowly pulled out. "Thank you," he said then got off the bed. He walked towards the bathroom.

"Your turn," Lisa told Daniel. She increased her pace and stared at him. She licked her lips and gave him a come hither look.

In one motion he grabbed her, flipped her onto her back and re-entered her. He rode her hard and fast.

Glen came back from the washroom with a couple of towels and saw the speed that Daniel was going. "Wow. Rocket man," he said. "Ride her hard and fast. She likes that."

Kelly leaned up and kissed Daniel. The thought of having a mini three way was overpowering and he felt the cum build inside of him. He came and collapsed onto Lisa.

"He's down," Kelly said.

Glen handed her a towel.

Daniel rolled off Lisa who got up and went to the washroom.

"That was fun," Kelly said.

"It was," Glen said. "We should do it again."

Kelly smiled. "I would like that."

Glen went to the desk and wrote on a piece of paper. "Here is our email," Glen said, handing it to Daniel.

"Let me give you our email," Kelly said.

On the way home, Daniel asked Kelly what she thought and she said, "It was great. I really like them."

"Yes. I think that we have found a replacement for Viktor and Vera."

"Oh yeah, them. I forgot about our old Russian friends. I guess that is a good sign of how good it was."

"Yes."

"Did you like Lisa?"

"Hell yes. Fun."

"I thought that I heard you say great tits."

"I did. I heard you say something about a big dick."

"I did. God was he hung." She smiled.

"Slut."

"Yep. I hope that we see them again."

"Me too."

A Swinging Couple

Chapter Seven:
Eight Is Enough

Kelly got an email from Lisa inviting them to a club on Saturday. She had never heard of the Red Hot Spa before so she clicked the link that Lisa included. To her it looked classy and she liked the hot tub and pool.

Lisa also mentioned that they had invited two other couples and if something happened then great. Kelly showed it to Daniel who said, "Why not go and see what happens? Even if we don't like them we still like Glen and Lisa."

"That is what I was thinking."

"Okay, let's try it."

Kelly wore little black dress and was pretty sure that she wouldn't be wearing that for very long.

The club's entrance was in an alley and if you didn't know it was there, you would never spot it. They walked in and came to a desk. "Good evening," the man said. He was middle aged and smiling. "First time here?"

"Yes," Daniel said.

The man explained the rules of the club which

were basically the same as all the other clubs that Daniel and Kelly had been to. What was different was the entrance fee. "It is eighty dollars per couple."

Ouch, Kelly thought as Daniel opened his wallet.

The man hit a button that opened the door. It swung open to reveal a short staircase.

Inside was a bar on the left side with a dozen of tables and two openings for hallways on the right. There were three couples there and they all glanced up to see Kelly coming down the stairs. She was certainly checked out. This made her feel sexy.

A middle aged woman was waiting for them and said, "If you are ready, I can give you a tour."

"Sure."

Down the first hallway was the door to the outdoor pool and she said, "The pool is heated."

"Good. It isn't exactly warm out today."

The next door was for the hot tub. They looked in and saw three people in the hot tub. They walked down the hall passed the bathroom and came to a stairway. At the top of the stairs was a change room. "We ask you to change when you come upstairs. Only towels are permitted from this point on."

From there were five doorways. One led to another bar, one to the washroom and the others were for the playrooms. They went into one. It had three beds and a large couch. This room was connected to the next that was basically one big bed. The final room was a smaller room with just one bed in it.

Upstairs were the private rooms and the TV room. "There is a camera aimed at the bed for those who want to share their experience with everyone."

"Ah, not for us," Kelly said.

Daniel laughed.

The woman said, "It isn't for me either, but some people are into it."

"Some are," Daniel muttered.

"Well that is the end of the tour," the woman said. "I will show you how to get back downstairs to the bar."

"Thank you," Kelly said. "It looks like a very nice club."

Daniel and Kelly found a spot at the end of the bar by the wall and ordered a drink. It was eight o'clock and that was the time that they were suppose to meet. Ten minutes later, there was still no sign of Glen and Lisa. A couple came in and got the attention of Daniel and Kelly. She wore a tight white dress that hung onto her svelte body. She was definitely in shape. He was handsome and had a good built. They took a seat at the middle of the bar.

Another couple came in and again, Kelly was disappointed that it wasn't Glen and Lisa. This couple wasn't as good looking as the first, but they were still attractive. She was busty and had long black hair. They made a beeline straight for the other couple and it was apparent that they all knew each other.

Ten minutes and another drink later, Glen and Lisa finally made their appearance. When they walked in and went to the foursome, Kelly and Daniel knew that they were the other two couples that Lisa had mentioned.

"Oh this could be fun," Daniel whispered.

"Let's go over."

Glen gave Kelly a peck and shook Daniel's hand. Lisa gave them both kisses and introduced them to the other four. The other two couples were Chad and Linda and Frank and Mary. Kelly was attracted to Frank, but she was really turned on by

Chad and Glen. I am already ready to go, right now, she thought.

As Kelly and Glen were deep in conversation, Daniel tried to talk to Lisa, but she seemed more interested in talking with Chad. To him, she seemed a little aloof. However, Linda was more than interested in talking to him and he admired her body as they spoke. This wasn't lost on her.

The four of them walked up to the first play room and Glen sat down on the couch. Kelly sat beside him. She was so close to him that she was touching him. There was no doubt that she couldn't wait to have his dick inside of her.

Lisa sat on the chair and Daniel sat on the bed beside Linda who didn't mind. In fact, she encouraged it by talking about how her job kept in shape. "Being a letter carrier has its perks," she said. "I don't have to go to the gym to get my exercise."

The way that she looked at him, told him that he could take her right then and there.

"We all should go up to the change room," Glen told Lisa.

They braved the cold and went outside to the pool.

Glen and Lisa dropped their towels and went in. The other two couples were already in. Kelly followed and was quickly in the pool. "It is warm," she told Daniel who dropped his towel and went in.

Seeing that the other four were busy in the shallow end, Kelly and Daniel swam over to Glen and Lisa who were at the side of the pool where the deep end started. Kelly moved towards Glen who said, "Come."

Glen and Kelly swam away leaving Daniel to play with Lisa.

Now she is game, he thought.

Glen and Kelly made out at the side of the pool and she enjoyed having his large hands on her body. At first he played with her ass, then he touched her clit. He flickered it while his kissed her. While kissing him back, she reached down and grabbed his cock.

I love this thing, she thought and felt a little guilty about liking it more than Daniel's.

Glen's cock was bigger by about twenty-five percent and it took her to her limit of expansion. Well, it stretched her more than any other cock had stretched her before.

Big big cock, she thought. Such a nice big cock.

Their kissing was interrupted when Glen felt a presence behind him. The other four people were leaving the pool.

"We should go to the hot tub now," he said to her.

The dash from the pool to the indoors was cold and all eight of them didn't hesitate to go into the hot tub to warm up.

The room for the hot tub was well lit, too well lit. Kelly felt a little exposed and shy about sitting there naked. A guy with two large women were at the other end of the pool so that brought the total of eleven people in the hot tub. It was pretty crowded and after she had warmed up Kelly wanted to go.

A number of them were talking about another club, but she barely listened. She wanted to fuck and just sitting around was boring her. She was happy that Daniel spotted this and asked her, "Warmed up yet."

"Oh yeah," she said. "I am pretty hot."

"That you are," Glen said.

"Thanks."

"Enough foreplay," Glen said. "Shall we all go upstairs?"

All agreed.

Chapter Eight:
Orgy

The other two couples had already moved into the room and Kelly and Lisa were talking outside. Daniel came and interrupted their conversation by asking, "Why aren't you two kissing?" He laughed.

"Good idea," Lisa.

With only towels wrapped around them, the two women embraced in a long passionate kiss. Glen arrived and he was smiling. "If you two aren't too busy," he said, "maybe we should go in."

They walked into to see that both beds were occupied. Frank was onto top of Linda fucking her on the bed to the left while Mary was giving head to Chad on the other bed.

"Nice," Daniel said.

Glen sat down on the bench and Kelly sat right beside him. Lisa sat beside her with Daniel sitting to her left. The girls started kissing and Kelly cupped one of Lisa's large tits. Lisa shifted positions so that she could go down on Kelly. Kelly gladly spread her legs.

While the girls were getting busy, Glen moved over to the bed where Mary and Chad were. Then he went to the other bed.

The German couple that Kelly and Daniel had dance with a few months back came into the room and started fucking on the unoccupied bed. Daniel didn't have a problem with that and no one else noticed. It is an orgy so who can I stop from fucking near me, he thought.

The girls were finished and Kelly saw that Linda was giving Glen head and got a little jealous. She went over and offered to help her. They took turns sucking him, which he didn't object to.

Daniel put on a condom and he had a problem. He wasn't as hard as he should have been. Damn condoms, he thought. Okay, think of what is happening here.

He looked around and started to get hard. Good, he is coming back.

He slid it in and started to pump Lisa. She moved her butt to take as much of him as she could. Unfortunately, a fat couple came in and stood at the edge of the bed where Kelly was. They were waiting to be invited onto the bed. Kelly and Glen saw this and ignored them. Daniel saw them and was instantly turned off. He lost his erection.

Damn, he cursed.

The fat couple went over and stood by the other bed where Chad and Mary were fucking. They too ignored them. Then they went to the German couple and the German guy shook his head.

Daniel pulled out and was about to go down on Lisa when she got up and went to the bed where Chad and Mary were. She started kissing Mary.

Alone, Daniel went to the chair between the beds and sat down. To his left, Linda was being pumped by Chad, while Kelly was sucking Glen's oversized cock.

Linda came over with a condom and put it onto Daniel's penis. Then she sat on it and rode hard. "Easy girl," he told her with a smile on his face.

Meanwhile Kelly went over to a kneeling Chad and laid down on her stomach in front of him. She took his cock into her mouth. Glen came behind her and somehow managed to slide his cock into her pussy. It was a tight fit and Kelly moaned with pleasure.

After a few minutes, Chad left to go play with Lisa's ass that had been staring him in the face ever since she had come onto the other bed. Linda took his spot and got down on all fours. Daniel slid into her, admiring her ass.

It might be even better than Kelly's, he thought.

Not sure, maybe I will do a side by side comparison.

Kelly rolled over onto her back and Glen put his cock back inside of her. She reached over between Linda's legs and played with her clit. She must have been touching the right spot because Linda jerked violently and forced Daniel's cock out of her. As she did she squirted all over Kelly's hand.

Daniel slid back in and after Kelly wiped her hand off, she started to play with the other woman's clit again. After a few minutes, Linda again jerked violently, evicting Daniel's cock and squirting all over Kelly's hand.

"Again," Kelly said. "Wow."

"Let's go for a third time," Linda said.

They repositioned themselves and after a few minutes, Linda exploded for a third time.

"I am impressed," Kelly said. "Three orgasms in one session."

"Five. I had two earlier."

Kelly glared at the other woman. These people are hard core swingers, she thought. They take fucking very seriously.

Kelly lay on her back with her legs spread. Glen

got between them and re-entered.

Without warning, Glen picked up Kelly and took her to the couch where he lay her down on her back. He got between her legs and started to play with her clit.

Daniel looked over and saw that Kelly was enjoying herself. She was being massaged in all the right spots by a guy she had the hot's for. He was a little jealous and really turned on by the way she was taking all the pleasure that he could give her. Unfortunately, he was too turned on by this and started humping like mad.

"I think that you are going to cum," Linda told him.

She was right and his cock released a load of cum a dozen strokes later.

When they got home Daniel threw Kelly onto the bed and she asked, "What are you doing?"

"I am going to fuck you."

"Didn't you get enough?"

"Yes, but I never had you."

"But you have me all the time."

"I know. That is what makes me a happy man."

Part Two:

The

Orgy

Club

Chapter One:
Parking

Kelly Ferguson felt herself slipping away into reckless abandonment; passion was winning control over her young body. A few hours ago the petite redhead couldn't picture herself in the backseat of a car being felt up by a complete stranger. The fact that the complete stranger was handsome helped. Actually, it was the only reason why she was doing this. She clinched her eyes and absorbed that special feeling when sex feels ten times better than it normally did. His fingers touched all the right spots as he nuzzled her neck. Her nipples strained against her blouse in a desperate play for attention. He slipped a finger inside of her to soak up the moisture before he went back to her clit, lightly teasing the tip of it. This drove her wild. She rocked with passion, throwing her arms around him and squeezing tighter and tighter the closer that she approached orgasm. His mouth found one of her nipples and played with it through her blouse. His movements softly rubbed her silk bra against her nipples adding to the pleasure. When he intensified his rhythm it was too much to take and with her back arched, she exploded.

Once her orgasm had finished, he repositioned her and slid his cock into her wet pussy. Kelly liked that. She couldn't remember the name of this guy who was fucking her and that turned her on. To her, he was just a piece of meat and she wanted more.

Meanwhile, in the car next to the one that Kelly was being fucked in, Daniel was in the backseat riding a blonde with big tits. Her skirt had been hiked up and her bare legs were wrapped around Daniel's body as he humped her vigorously. Her blouse was open and her bra was on the floor. Her natural tits were flat against her body and to Daniel were the biggest that he had ever seen. Well, the biggest of any woman he had been with.

He was in love with Kelly and as much as he lusted after her svelte little body and pretty face, he sometimes needed to be with a large pair of tits. For some reason they had power over him. It was one of the reasons why they went to the club to pick up other couples. The other reason was that Kelly was a promiscuous little slut that got turned on by every handsome guy who crossed her path; and he did mean every handsome guy. So with her insatiable appetite for fresh cock and his need for big tits, swinging was perfect for them.

Daniel decided that he was approaching the finish

line so he rode her as fast as he could. The car rocked with their rhythm and she hung on to him as the pleasure built inside of both of them.

"Oh my god," he heard a voice say and then realized that it was his own.

After every drop of cum had left his body, he collapsed onto the next to the lady with the big tits. He looked out the window and saw that the car next to his was really rocking.

Kelly is getting her brains fucked out, he thought and was a little jealous that maybe the guy was better than him.

Inside the rocking car, Kelly hung onto the handsome man as his cock repeatedly rammed into her.

"Cum for me baby," she said and the guy somehow found another gear. He rode her quickly until he cried out with pleasure. It was all that Kelly could do but to hang on and take the pleasure until he stopped.

Kelly and Daniel arrived home and she was still horny. "God, that was fun," she said. "I want you to show me exactly what you did to her."

"Okay."

"Let's pretend that the chesterfield is the backseat of my car," she said and then sat down.

"Actually, I was on the left, or your side."

She got up and moved to the other side of him. "Now what?"

"Then I took her like this."

"Don't speak, just fuck me."

With his arms around her, he kissed her firmly. She kissed back with equal passion and she liked being controlled. His hand cupped her tit and she moaned. He lifted her blouse and his lips and tongue found her nipple. She let her head fall back and with her eyes closed she caressed the back of his head. She liked this even more when she felt his hand slide between her legs. The sensation of her tits and in particular her nipple, was enhanced by a finger being slipped between her pussy lips. At first he fucked her with one finger then he inserted a second one.

"More! More! More!" She shouted.

He inserted a third finger and she rocked her lips to help him fuck her. He felt how wet she was and wondered if she was going to cum.

Her hand slipped down and she quickly rubbed her clit.

Yep, he thought, she is going to cum.

He fucked her with his fingers as quickly as she could and waited.

Her body jerked and his fingers got even wetter. She came all over them. He pulled them out and licked his fingers. He loved the way she smelled and tested.

"Fuck me!" She told him.

Because of his boner, he could barely get his pants off. He slid into her and wasted no time. He fucked her hard.

"I love you," she called out. "You'll always be my favorite."

Hearing those words he got stiffer than he had been all night and she felt the extra growth.

"Come for me baby," she said in his ear.

A Swinging Couple

Chapter Two:
If This Boat is Rocking

Kelly and Daniel boarded the boat at the marina and were greeted by two sexy people in daring swim wear. Laura's bikini was super tight and her sexy body made the expression, camel toes, pop into Daniel's mind. He licked his lips as he could almost taste her pussy. He wondered if the carpet matched the drapes and if she was a real blonde or not. Her hair was bleached and he knew that her white hair wasn't her natural color, but her eyebrows looked pretty fair so he figured that she probably had started life off as a blonde. Her breasts were perky and he figured were 36 C cup. Her hips were round and inviting.

Cliff's look was even more shameless. The Speedo that the banking executive wore was also very tight and Kelly could see the outline of the handsome man's cock head. She knew that he had been circumcised.

Their boat was big enough to have a few benches and a bar below and Kelly knew that her and Daniel were doing a little bit of social climbing by befriending Cliff and Laura. He had money and this boat showed that fact off.

"I'm glad that you two could make it," Laura said.

"Nice boat," Kelly said. She looked at Cliff and added, "Or is it a yacht?

Cliff smiled, "It isn't big enough to be a yacht, but you my dear, can call it anything you want to."

Kelly swore that she saw the head of his cock move. Judging by the way that he stared at her, she was pretty sure that his cock was interested in her.

"Did you bring your swimsuits," Laura asked. She saw that Daniel was wearing his trunks and a t-shirt. Kelly was in a pair of cut-off shorts and a t-shirt.

"Underneath," Kelly said.

"You can go take them off downstairs. Come."

Kelly followed Laura down the steps and couldn't help looking at her ass cheeks as they spilled out from the black bikini bottom.

"I'm glad that you two came. We don't party at the club. It is too public for us."

"We are overjoyed to be invited."

"Before anything happens, do you two have any restrictions?"

Kelly shook her head.

"Hard swaps?"

Kelly smiled. "Is there any other kind?"

"Bisexuality?"

"Oh yes please." Kelly smiled and then laughed. As Laura watched, she dropped her shorts and took of her t-shirt. She wore a black bikini that wasn't as skimpy as Laura's, but like Laura's, it showed off her thin, but curvy body.

They heard the motor start and Laura said, "Looks like Cliff isn't the only one that is in a hurry to get things started."

Kelly looked at her like she wanted to be kissed.

"Relax honey, when we anchor at the island, we will have time to play. Come, let's get some sun on the forward deck."

Cliff anchored just off and as the drinks were being served, another boat came into view. Laura looked up and said, "That looks like Mike and Debbie."

Who is that? Kelly wondered and wasn't happy with the interruption. Hopefully, they just came to say hello and then fuck off.

A boat that was a little smaller than Cliff's came along side and anchored. It was quite apparent that both Mike and Debbie spent a lot of time in the gym. Both were muscle bound and tanned. They too were wearing skimpy outfits that left nothing to the imagination.

"They own a gym," Laura said to Kelly.

"No kidding."

"I swear that she is gay, but won't admit it. The last time we were with them she spent most of her time between my legs."

They came aboard. Debbie was short and her shoulders and arms were thicker than most men's. Her hair was dark brown and her overly tanned face was roundish, suggesting an Asian influence. Her body was well toned from top to bottom. There was not one ounce of fat on her body. She looked like a miniature version of Mike, except that Mike didn't have an Asian look that Debbie had. He too didn't have an ounce of fat on his body and Kelly stared at his biceps. Each one was the size of her head.

"Do you mind if they join us?" Laura whispered to Kelly and Daniel. "We've partied with them before."

Kelly and Daniel looked at each other and shrugged. "Sure," Kelly said, "The more the merrier."

Laura said, "Everyone come in for some drinks." She walked down the steps into a room where there was a bar on one side, a bench on the other end and a bench directly ahead. The benches were patted, deep and comfy. They were more like sofas than benches.

Kelly sat on the bench directly in front and Mike sat beside her. Laura grabbed Daniel's hand and led him to the other bench. Debbie sat down beside him and Daniel found himself between two women. Cliff sat down beside Kelly so that she had a man on each side of her.

"Well, this is cozy," Daniel said.

"It certainly is," Cliff said laughing.

Kelly felt a hand on each one of her legs. Both men were caressing her smooth skin and her breathing became more deliberate as she anticipated being double teamed. She looked at Daniel and saw that basically the same thing was happening to him. The women's hands were all over his body. Laura went in for a kiss and Daniel happily obliged. As she watched her man make-out with another woman a hand touched her pussy through her bikini while another hand touched her stomach and was moving up to her breasts. Two more hands were on her now and she leaned her head back and closed her eyes. She surrendered and she knew that she didn't have to do a thing. She knew that the two horny guys that were feeling her up will take care of it all. She felt her bikini come off and someone parted her legs.

She moaned when Mike's tongue touched her pussy lips. Cliff kissed her other lips and she let her tongue play with his tongue. Her hand found Cliff's cock. It was hard and she played with it through the fabric.

Meanwhile Daniel's cock was in Laura's mouth and his tongue was in Debbie's mouth. His hands were all over her body and he felt a little strange. Parts of her were like a woman and parts were like a man. Her arms and shoulders were very strong. He undid her top and she moved forward so that her left tit was in his face. His right hand touched her between her legs and he wouldn't have been surprised to discover that she had a dick. Instead his hand found a soft wet pussy. She took off her bikini bottom to allow him to touch her better. The strong woman melted like any other woman when he played with her clit.

Laura put a condom on him and sat on it.

This is good, Daniel thought. I have a hot blonde riding my cock, my hand I splaying with a clean shaven pussy of another woman and I have a nice tit in my face.

Debbie's arms were around Laura and the women kissed.

Kelly was also in a good place. Mike was between her legs still eating her and Cliff's cock was in her mouth. It was a good size and Kelly's left hand hung onto to the base of it while she sucked the rest of it.

Mike put his cock into her and she enjoyed being double teamed.

I love cock! She thought.

Debbie got up and went to the bag that she had brought. She pulled out a strap-on and put it on. She tapped Mike on the shoulder and told him to move. He went to the opposite side of Cliff and put his cock in Kelly's face. Kelly grabbed it with her right hand and she now had two cocks in her hands.

Debbie put her head into Kelly's crotch and licked. It was good. Kelly had always liked the softness of a woman's touch and, it was obvious that Debbie was very experienced with women. Debbie did what Mike couldn't, and that was to give Kelly an orgasm.

Daniel heard her and watched as he fucked Laura. He had the natural blonde in the missionary position on the bench.

Kelly wasn't prepared for the dildo that Debbie shoved into her.

Three cocks, she thought. Two real ones, one fake. The biggest one is cliff's followed by the dildo then Mike.

Mike left and went over and tapped Daniel on the shoulder. "Switch," he said.

Mike took over fucking Laura and Daniel went behind Debbie. He put on a fresh condom and eased his cock into her pussy. He fucked the woman who was fucking Kelly. She was really tight and he looked at her muscular back. Then he watched Kelly slurp on Cliff's dick.

He's hung, Daniel thought. And my little girl is in lust.

Debbie kissed Kelly's cheek and moaned forward her lips. She stopped sucking to make-out with her. He put a condom on. Debbie pulled the strap-on out of Kelly and Cliff swung her around so that she was lying on the bench. He glided into her. Daniel continued to hump Debbie as she made out with Kelly.

Kelly felt lost in lust and she loved it. She had been riding a wave of pleasure since Debbie made her cum. She made of point of remembering to thank her later for that.

Debbie left and once again told her husband to move. She rammed the dildo into Laura. Daniel waved his cock in Laura's face and she took it. Mike went to do the same to Kelly, but she had all four limbs wrapped around Cliff and the two of them were making out. So, he took Debbie from behind.

Cliff and Kelly got into a good rhythm and his came. He lay motionless on her as they watched the others. He pulled out and sat up. Kelly did too. Both of them were content.

Mike indicated to Daniel to switch and they did. However, instead of entering Debbie right away, Daniel pulled her off Laura and threw her on her back. He held her legs apart and entered her. The dildo pointed straight up and rubbed against his body. He rode her hard until he came. Mike did the same to Laura.

After everyone had recovered, the subject of jealously was raised and Cliff added his two cents worth by saying, "Two women playing with each other is the swinger's safety net, no one gets jealous over their woman getting it on with another woman. This was all too apparent the first time that we braved a swinger's club. From our seat in a dark corner, we eyed the dozen or so couples on the dance floor, three of them females couples in various stages of undressing and/or pawing each other. I wanted in, but I also didn't want to see my wife join in."

"It takes a little getting used to," Daniel said. "But now I like it when she gets into it."

Cliff said, "Yeah! Kelly certainly got into it today."

"And every day."

Kelly shook her head. "Boys!"

"Come on, you mean to tell me that you wouldn't want to do this on a regular basis?"

She couldn't argue with him because she knew that he was right.

"I would love to do this on a regular basis," Laura said. "We should start a club."

Kelly really liked that idea.

Chapter Three:
A New Fantasy

A petite redhead with short cropped hair that highlighted a pretty face was on a couch watching TV with her husband. Actually her mind was wandering too much to constitute watching TV. She was more glancing at the set as her eyes wandered.

"I like orgies," Kelly blurted out loud. "All those limbs and sexual organs interconnecting…" She licked her lips. "So hot."

She opened her pants and slid her hand down her panties. Her finger rubbed between her pussy lips. She sighed and closed her eyes.

"I guess that you do like them," Daniel said. He watched his wife masturbate.

"Fuck yeah." She moaned and her breathing matched her hips as they rocked.

"Who would you invite to our orgy?" He asked while watching her fuck herself. He unzipped his pants and took out his erect penis.

With her eyes clinched she said, "Cliff and Laura, Mike and Debbie of course…" She moaned.

"Who else?"

"I don't know."

He rubbed his penis in her face. "Mmm, a hard man is good to fine," she said. "I want more of these in my life. "She opened her mouth.

"Okay and how do you want to do that?"

On her feet was a pair of black stilettos, which her thin feet looked good in. Her calves were thin, her thighs were smooth and her round ass was barely covered by her black mini-skirt. Her stomach was flat and uncovered. Her belly button was small and Kelly wanted to pour wine into it and lick it out with her tongue. Her breasts were small and perky and only covered by a colorful tube top. Her arms and shoulders were bare and thin and on a thin neck was one of the prettiest faces that Kelly had ever seen. Her hair was long, thick and dark red.

Kelly was immediately impressed and jealous of this woman. She knew that she was Daniel's type. He liked his women petite, pretty and promiscuous, three things that Kelly knew that she was and she didn't want the competition. Needless to say, it was a good jpeg.

The next picture was of the perfect woman's

husband. Kelly was immediately attracted to him. Broad shoulders, strong arms and a fatless body. He was in shape and Kelly had thoughts about having him between her legs. She wondered what his cock was like.

They must look great together, she thought and pictured him and her in a few sexual positions.

"They look good," Daniel said. "Are they in the club?"

"Not sure, we are just going to have to meet them for a try-out."

He smiled. "Oh yeah."

Kelly was a little jealous of the way he looked at the other woman. She cringed when he asked, "What is that pretty thing's name?"

"They are…" she scrolled down to see. "Trevor and Ethel."

"No, that can't be. She doesn't look like an Ethel."

"Why? How many Ethels do you know?"

"None, but…"

"Oh, my mistake. Wrong couple. "Karl and Crystal."

"Crystal. Nice."

Kelly looked over her shoulder and was eye level with his crotch. She reached over and felt that he was semi-hard. "God, a picture of her turns you on. She may be a huge bitch and you wouldn't want to stick this into her."

"I don't care. All I have to do is fuck her, not live with her."

"Still the chemistry may be wrong."

"That is why we are meeting them."

"That's true."

"So, what did your ad say?"

"Hang on, I'll bring it up."

She pointed to the screen and it read: "We are looking for hot couples who are into hard swaps to join an orgy club. We will meet once a month. We are only looking for a few couples right now. If interested please email us a picture at the address above. Daniel and Kelly."

"So were are really going through with this?"

"I can't think of a reason why not. We will try it and if we don't like it we will bail."

"Is there anyone else?"

"Funny you should ask. Tonight we are meeting

David and Amy for drinks."

"And sex?"

"Probably not."

"Oh." He looked disappointed.

"Anyhow, I am going to book a hotel room where we will have our first meeting. I am thinking of the Marriott."

"Nice. Who is paying for this?"

"You are." She laughed. "Don't worry a few people have already said that they will chip in."

"How big is the room?"

"A normal size I guess."

"Will it be big enough?"

"It has two king size beds in it."

"That's five people per bed."

She smiled. "Nice and cozy."

"When are we meeting Karl and Crystal?"

"Not sure. They are pretty busy."

David and Amy were waiting for them on the patio of the bar. She was chesty and her big tits are what

Daniel noticed as they approached the table. He also noticed that her hair was long and brown and that she was tall and thin.

"Are they real?" Kelly asked.

"Who cares?" He asked sarcastically.

Kelly rolled her eyes. "Pervert."

"Yep."

"Well, he is cute."

He was also tall and thin and his hair was brown.

"Hello David and Amy," Kelly said.

Their greeting was friendly and they were invited to sit. After a few minutes of small talk, Daniel asked, "How long have you two been in the life-style?"

Kelly had already asked them a bunch of questions during their online chat so she already knew that answer.

"About a year," David said. "And you guys?"

Before either Daniel or Kelly could answer, Amy asked. "Is this an audition?"

Kelly smiled and told her, "You've already passed that. You two are too good looking not to have in the club." The way that she looked at David told everyone at the table that she was really attracted to him and that she wanted to fuck him. "We are having our inaugural meeting next Saturday. Do you want to attend?"

"Yes, we would love to."

"Ever been to an orgy?"

"No. Just one couple at a time."

The waitress came by and they ordered another round.

"Excuse me," Kelly said getting up.

"I'll go with you," Amy said and got up too.

In the Ladies' room, Kelly asked Amy if she was up to this and then added, "Orgies can be very intense. I love them, but not everyone does. It is a free-for-all and the last time we were with two other couples I had a cock in each hand and Debbie fucked me with a strap-on." She peered at Amy in order to gage her reaction.

"That sounds like a lot of fun," Amy said. "I want to try that."

"How much girl-on-girl have you done?"

"Some, but we've had a lot of threesome with other guys. I am used to having a prick in each hand."

Kelly nodded. "Okay, I think you're ready."

"I'm excited." She smiled at Kelly who took it as an invitation to kiss her. After a minute of playing with each other's tongues, she said, "We should stop in case someone comes in," Kelly said. "We can continue this somewhere else."

"We can't at our place. My mother is watching the kids."

"Then it is our place."

Neither of the men protested the change in location.

In the kitchen, Daniel opened the fridge and pulled out four beers. When he brought them into the living room the women were busy making out on the sofa.

"I want to be fucked with a strap-on as I have two dicks in my mouth," Amy said.

"But I don't have one," Kelly said. "We'll make sure that Debbie brings her toys. She will love you. In the meantime, I could eat you as the boys put their dicks in your mouth. How does that sound to you?"

Without warning Amy pushed Kelly onto the sofa.

It was gentle, but firm. Kelly didn't protest. Amy lifted Kelly's dress and pulled off her panties.

"You are not wasting time, are you?"

"Show me how it is done first," Amy said and then went down on Kelly as the men struggled out of their pants. Daniel was the first one to have his big cock in her face and she waited for David to get naked. She beamed when she saw his cock. "Oh my god," she blurted. "You're hung."

Circumstances dictated that it was impossible for Daniel and Kelly to swing with Karl and Crystal before the first Orgy Club meeting. However, they did have time to meet up for drinks on the Wednesday before.

Kelly was a little taken back about the way that Daniel looked at Crystal. Yes, they have been with beautiful women before, but there was something different about this one. She felt that this woman was competition for her husband's affections.

As a result she might have been a little too harsh with them. Kelly asked, "Are you both sure that you are up for this? It will be, well, nothing will be held back and it won't be casual. We don't want anybody freaking out or anything like that. We don't want any duds. They wreck the mood."

Karl and Crystal looked at each other. "I think that we are good," Karl said.

"You think or do you know?"

"We know."

Daniel tried to relieve the tension by saying, "Good. We are glad that you're in."

As Crystal and Kelly glared at each other, Karl asked Daniel, "Is there going to be a charge or anything?"

"No, but if you chip in for the room, it will be very much appreciated."

"That won't be a problem."

Crystal looked into Kelly's eyes and told her, "Don't worry. We are experienced and won't be a dud."

"Okay."

Daniel cut in and said to Crystal, "Sorry, we had to check."

Afterwards, Daniel asked her why she was so rough on them. She replied, "I don't like having unknowns in the group, this being our first meeting and all."

"I am sure that they will be fine. If they are not then we will ask them to leave."

"That could be awkward. Excuse me, fuck or get out. I don't want it to get to that point."

"I am sure that it won't. Like they said, they are experienced swingers. They might have done more than us."

She scuffed. "I find that hard to believe. We've been married now for only two months and we have already slept with five couples. And don't ask me to count how many people we fucked before we got married. Christ, we even hooked up with another couple on our honeymoon."

He smiled. "It has been fun."

She looked at them. "I think that we shouldn't include Karl and Crystal this time."

"Um, no. We have already invited them. We can't uninvited them. That would be…well, I doubt that they would come to the next one, purely out of spite."

"But…"

"I'll tell you what. Let me handle it. If they are duds then I will make sure they leave. So you don't have to worry about it, okay?"

She didn't answer it. "Who is the leader of the group?"

"Me," Daniel said playfully.

She glared at him, which caused him to snicker. Then he added. "But since you are in charge of me, you are in overall command."

"It was my idea for the group."

Seriously he said, "Yes, but it is our group. It is something that we do together."

"Yes." She walked away and he knew that something wasn't good with her.

He thought about going after her to hear what the problem was or wondered if he should just let her deal with it herself.

"Ugh," he groaned.

He found her at the computer in the den and squatted down beside her.

"Well, it is done," she said.

"Um, what is done?" He was worried that she had just kicked Karl and Crystal out of the group.

"I booked the room and emailed all the members of the Orgy Club."

"Oh, and they are?"

"Cliff and Laura, Mike and Debbie, David and Amy and Karl and Crystal. And us, of course."

He nodded. "Okay, good. Ten people, one room. Should be interesting."

She sighed. "I just hope that it all goes well."

"Me too. Nervous?"

"Yes."

"Well, if it all goes wrong, we still have each other."

She rested her head against his shoulder. "Yes."

For the first time Kelly doubted what she was doing.

"Excuse me," she said and walked into the washroom.

She thought, I have actually arranged for ten people to meet in a hotel room under my name for the sole purpose of getting naked and having sex with each other. This is not usual behavior. Granted, I have already fucked seven of the nine people that will be there, but…

Crystal. That what was bothering her. She was the only other woman that she hadn't been with so she was an unknown. She also hated Daniel's reaction to her and considered asking him not to touch her

115

at the orgy.

"I can't do that," she muttered to herself. "That's unfair."

Maybe, she thought, she will be a total stiff and Daniel will be bored by her.

She looked at her wedding ring and reminded herself that Daniel and her were in a committed relationship and that they were very happy together.

So why did she fear losing him?

She found him on the sofa and cuddled back with him. "Hey," she said nonchalantly, trying to be cool.

"Hey," he answered back, matching her coolness.

"Please tell me that I have nothing to worry about with Crystal?"

"Don't worry, they will be fine once the action starts. They will join right in. I don't expect that they will start it, but you never know."

"No, I mean..."

"Oh, so that is it. You are threatened by her."

"Um, no..."

"Yes you are, but don't worry. I might fuck her and

that's it."

"It's an orgy; chances are you will fuck her."

"True, but you never know at these things. I might not have the opportunity to do her."

"I hope you don't." She looked at Daniel. "Sorry, I didn't mean that."

"Oh yes you did. Why are you threatened? David has a bigger dick that I do and I'm not threatened."

"Not much bigger. You're both really hung."

He smiled. "Why thank you."

She rolled her eyes and tried not to smile at his silliness. "It is your reaction to her that bugs me. You make a fuss over how good she looks."

"That is the same way that I make a fuss over you. That's because you are both something special. I was so into you and I still am."

"So you admit that I have something to worry about!"

"No! She is with Karl and you are with me. We will fuck – hopefully – but that's all. I'm with you and that is the final word. Christ I married you didn't I?"

She could tell that he was becoming irritated by her

petty jealousy and that he was right; anything that happened between him and Crystal was temporary.

"I'm sorry," she said.

"No problem. You know how to thank me," he joked.

She thought, why not?"

Her left hand unzipped his pants and she leaned forward.

"I was joking," he said. His cock was getting harder by the second.

"I know, but you are not trying to stop me either. Want me to swallow?"

"Yes." He leaned back and closed his eyes.

That caused him to be fully erect. He moaned when her lips touched his cock her tongue licked the sides of it and she went up and down on it.

"You're the best," he said.

He reached out and put his hand on her beautiful little ass. He pictured how much attention it was going to get on orgy night. It was easily the nicest ass of all the women in the group, except Crystal, he thought. It is possible that her ass might be nicer than Kelly's nice little rump.

Kelly's head bobbed on his cock and he was touching her ass, he thought about Crystal and the things that he wanted to do to her. He didn't get very far because his load flew out of his cock and straight down Kelly's throat.

A Swinging Couple

Chapter Four:
A Room For Ten Please

Kelly told the woman at the front desk of the Marriott that there would be two couples staying the night so she needed at least two keys. This wasn't a problem and as they waited, Daniel wondered why she had brought a suitcase with her. He knew better than to ask.

The other couple that was booked in with them was Cliff and Laura and once Kelly got the room number she texted them.

The room was fairly big. It had two beds and a sitting area with a small sofa, a chair and a table.

"What is the game plan?" Daniel said.

"We are all to meet in the bar downstairs at eight."

Kelly unpacked and Daniel asked," Why bother, if we are only here for one night?"

She ignored him.

There was a knock at the door and Daniel answered it. "What the hell do you want?" He said mockingly to Cliff.

"To fuck your wife."

"Well then, you had better come on in." He held the door for them.

"Hello fellow swinger," Laura said to Kelly and hugged her.

Kelly pointed at Laura's suitcase and gave Daniel a look. "Whatever," he said.

"What are you wearing," Laura asked Kelly.

"What are you wearing," Daniel asked Cliff sarcastically.

"I thought that I would wear my pink golf shirt."

"Oh the one with the nice ribbons. Nice."

"You guys," Laura said.

"Anyone for a pregame warm-up?" Daniel asked.

The women looked at each other and rolled their eyes.

Kelly wore a little black dress that showed off more leg than what was considered respectable.

Laura wore tight leather pants and a black t-shirt, which contrasted nicely with her white hair. The men wore slacks and a golf shirt, but neither of them wore pink. Daniel was in blue and Cliff was in green.

At ten to eight the four of them walked into the bar and eyed for a good place for ten of them to drink. Kelly saw it. In the corner sat a couple of empty sofas and two chairs arranged in a square. Kelly and Laura sat on a sofa, Cliff on another and Daniel took a chair.

"Who do you think will be the first ones to arrive?" Cliff asked.

No sooner had he said that then walked in to tall thin people.

"That's David and Amy," Kelly said to Laura and Cliff.

"Nice."

"It gets nicer once you see what is in his pants."

Laura gave Kelly a look.

"We had to audition them." Kelly smiled and then mouthed the words, `big'.

Daniel stood up and made the introductions just as the waitress came over to take their drink orders. The tall couple sat beside Cliff on the sofa.

Mike and Debbie came next and Debbie sat with Kelly and Laura on the sofa while Mike took the last chair. Karl and Crystal arrived fifteen minutes later and Daniel gave his seat to her. This did not go unnoticed by Kelly. She kept on eye on him as he stood and spoke to Karl.

After everyone had a drink, Kelly smiled and asked, "Is everyone finished?"

She heard a few people say, yes, and saw a number of nods. "Great. Then I think that it is time for all of us to go upstairs for our meeting."

Ten people more or less got up at once.

The elevator door opened and Daniel said, "Okay everyone, squeeze in."

The group barely got the door closed and Kelly felt someone's hand on her ass. She had no idea whose hand it was and that excited her. She placed her hand on Karl's back and rubbed his firm body.

Nice, she thought.

She heard a few giggles and knew that the other women were also being groped. The hand on her rubbed between her legs and she moaned. If she wasn't wet before she certainly was now. The elevator stopped at the tenth floor and the door opened.

"Aw," she said. "Fun ride is over."

Chapter Five:
Lustful Chaos

Ten people followed Daniel as he walked with card key in hand. "Here we are," he said, "Our room for the night."

He opened the door, walked in and threw the key onto the dresser. "Good, it is here," he said when he noticed a couple of bottles of champagne and ten glasses in a bucket.

Kelly was shocked and she looked at Daniel who said, "I had room service deliver it while we were downstairs."

"Nice touch."

Debbie and Laura sat on the first bed while Cliff took the chair and Mike sat on the other bed. Kelly sat beside Mike and watched the two newbie couples, Amy and David, take the sofa and Kelly called Karl and Crystal over. They sat at the end of the bed. Crystal was in front of her and watched Daniel open the champagne. Kelly was a little jealous. To her delight, Karl sat between Kelly and Crystal and smiled at her. The attention from him made her forget about Crystal.

Daniel noticed that Crystal was smiling at him. Her

blouse was open to a button below her ample breasts, revealing the soft curves of cleavage. He handed her the first glass of champagne.

"Do you want a drink?" David asked Kelly

"Sure," Kelly answered brightly.

Daniel handed Daniel and Amy a glass next because he wanted them to relax. They looked nervous. He saw that Karl had taken two glasses and handed one to Kelly. He also noticed that they were looking at each other lustfully. Next were Debbie and Laura who were cuddling on the first bed. Cliff was last.

"Okay, now that everyone has a drink," Daniel said. "Here is to our first meeting." He raised his glass. "Cheers!"

Glasses were clinched and the drinking began. He sat beside Crystal on the edge of the bed and said to her, "I can't let you sit here all by yourself."

"What a gentleman you are."

"Anything for a lady."

She rolled her eyes. "Lady, right," she said playfully. "I'm too much of a slut for that."

She raised an eyebrow and continued, "Look at my husband over there." He looked and saw him standing directly behind Laura with his hands around her waist. She was slowly grinding him. "He probably has a boner right now, which Laura seems to be enjoying."

"Yes, I think so."

"And look at Kelly sitting beside David. Too close."

Behind him Mike had slid over beside Kelly who had her legs draped over Karl. He rubbed her naked thighs. Kelly's legs automatically parted slowly, giving him a good view of her drenched pink panties.

Cliff said, "I find sexually liberated women a turn-on. Nothing is sexier than watching a good looking woman allow herself to be pleasured by whoever she wants to touch her."

Since Cliff was in deep conversation with Amy, David moved over to the bed where Debbie and Laura were making out. He watched Debbie's hands roam over Laura's body. Crystal saw that too. "Interesting party," she said to Daniel. She watched Cliff and Amy kiss. She turned around to see that Karl and Kelly were making out and that Mike was taking off her dress.

As Kelly made out with Mike, Karl moved between

her legs. Her panties were removed and replaced by Karl's tongue. His tongue added more moisture to an already damp spot. Kelly was really turned on and looked forward to an evening of un-abandoned lust. She was determined to fuck everyone in this room tonight; one night, nine lovers.

Karl slipped a couple of fingers into her pussy to help his tongue pleasure her.

One already, she thought as she felt an orgasm approach. She panted and opened her eyes enough to see Cliff suck on Amy's big and beautiful fake boobs. She licked her lips and made plans to play with both of them later.

Daniel was on top of Crystal on the end of the bed and right now she felt no jealousy. She was so turned on that he could do anything with anyone right now and she wouldn't care.

Mike dangled his cock in her face so she sucked on it.

All thoughts were lost as she was overtaken by an orgasm.

"We have the first orgasm of the night," Mike announced.

"Who?" Laura asked. She sounded disappointed

that it wasn't her.

"Kelly."

"Figures that it would be my wife the super slut," Daniel said, getting a number of laughs.

Kelly heard this, but she didn't care. A second orgasm was building. It startled her when Karl stopped to strip. As she slowly jerked Mike she studied Karl's strong body and licked her lips when he dropped his pants. She glared at his bulge.

"Fuck me," she told him.

Debbie and Laura were in a sixty-nine with Laura on top. David slid his oversized cock into Laura's pussy as Debbie's tongue played with her clit.

Daniel's tongue explored Crystal's pussy and he couldn't believe how beautiful the woman was. Every inch of her body was flawless and her pussy was no exception.

Her lips are amazing, he thought as he parted them with his hand.

As he ate her, he undressed himself. It was difficult getting his underwear off over his erection, but he found a way to get them off. He almost ripped them off.

Once he got a condom on, he couldn't wait any longer. He was as hard as he could be. He held her legs open and slid his cock into her. He was in Crystal, David was in Laura, Karl was in Kelly, Mike's cock was in Kelly's mouth and Cliff was preparing to mount Amy. With her ass on the edge of the sofa, she held out her legs so that Cliff had a great view of exactly where to stick his dick. She wrapped her long legs around him and pulled him closer until his dick slipped into her pussy.

Kelly was just about to suggest that Karl and Mike switch places when Karl came. It was quick. He sped up and grunted a lot. Mike took over right after. Now, with a clear view, she could see Daniel fuck Crystal and she didn't like it.

"Crystal, come here," she said. "I want to kiss you."

Daniel pulled out and Crystal crawled towards her. The two women kissed and Daniel admired Crystal's ass. He mounted her doggie style as she made out with his wife. Mike's hands roamed over Crystal's body.

"Pull me down," Kelly said to Mike. "I want Crystal to sit on my face."

"Hang on," Daniel said. He sped up and rode her hard until he came.

Crystal swung a leg over Kelly's head and lowered her butt until she felt Kelly's tongue on her pussy lips.

I'm doing the...I don't know what Karl and Crystal's last name is, Kelly thought. I'll just call them The Smiths. I'm doing the Smiths.

Mike enjoyed watching someone's wife being eaten by another woman and he liked it even more than his dick was inside of a woman that he barely knew. He thought about it and enjoyed the situation too much. Without warning cum flew out of his cock.

Two down, Kelly thought. Karl is done, Mike is done, Crystal is...close.

The beautiful woman squirmed and rocked her hips. Closer.

Kelly felt a cock enter her. She had no idea whose cock it was. Whoever it was, it felt good.

Crystal felt a pair of hands on her and turned to see that it was Cliff.

Daniel put his face between Amy's legs and she wrapped her long legs around his neck. Karl put his semi-hard cock in her face. He was slowly coming back and her lips wanted to help him make a full recovery.

Debbie kissed Crystal and she grabbed her tits. Cum from Laura's pussy was still on her lips and Crystal tasted it.

"Do you like the taste of pussy?" Debbie asked her.

She didn't give her a chance to respond because she shoved her tongue into her mouth. With Kelly's tongue doing wonders to her vagina, Cliff's hands touching her ass and tits, Debbie's hands on her tits and Debbie's lips on her, Crystal was overwhelmed with pleasure. She came over Kelly's tongue that was inserted halfway up her pussy at the time.

Three down, Kelly thought, I am a third of the way there.

Crystal got off Kelly's face and Kelly was pleasantly surprised to see that it was Cliff who had been riding her and was still fucking her.

Seeing the vacancy, Debbie was the next to sit on Kelly's face, only this time she faced Cliff so she could make out with him.

Another one bites the dust, Kelly thought when cliff came.

He was replaced by an unknown dick. It was a big one. Daniel or David? She wondered.

Kelly's tongue was getting a little tired so it came as a relief when Debbie had a nice little orgasm. Then she saw who was fucking her. Oh it is Daniel, she thought. "My husband is fucking me at an orgy. How romantic."

"What?" You were expecting flowers?"

She wrapped all four of her limbs around him and whispered in his ear, "Slow down."

They made love as others around them were getting their rocks off with other people's spouses. She had David, Laura and Amy left on her list, but she didn't care about it right now. Her man was inside of her and he wasn't looking anywhere else but at her.

"Slow down even more," she said.

He fucked her slowly.

She peered into his eyes and smiled. "I love you," she said.

"I do too."

"Now kiss me and gradually speed up."

He obeyed and during their long kiss they got into a solid rhythm. He got to a fairly fast pace and she panted. She hung on and her soft pussy felt every stroke from his hard cock.

She felt his load land inside of her. Neither one of them moved for the longest time. They could hear the other eight people get off around them. He rolled onto his back and she cuddled up to him.

"This club was a good idea," he said.

"Yes, it was."

"How long do you think this will last?"

"No idea. Most people are still going strong."

"No, I mean the club."

"At least one more meeting. Why, how long do you want it to last?"

"Until we are ninety I guess."

She laughed.

A few minutes later she asked, "Do you want to get back into the action?"

He didn't respond so she looked up. He was asleep.

"Is he asleep?" David asked her.

She saw him at the edge of the bed. His large cock was only half erect as it dangled from his body, but it was still an impressive size. "Yes. Do you want to put that in me?"

She rolled onto her back and spread her legs.

Laura knelt beside the bed and with her hand gently raised Daniel's flaccid cock. She put her lips around it and sucked on it. It slowly came back to life. Daniel felt pleasure and the bed move. He opened his eyes to see his cock in Laura's mouth and David between Kelly's legs. He was fucking her hard and fast and the bed shook with each powerful thrust. No romance just fucking, he thought as he watched them.

"You are back," Laura said.

She slipped a condom onto his dick and then squatted over him.

With Daniel inside of her, Laura leaned forward and instead of kissing Daniel she kissed Kelly instead. Kelly's hands cupped Laura's tits. Amy came along the other side and lay beside Kelly and nuzzled Kelly's neck as she made out with Laura.

The last three, Kelly thought. Perfect. Now to make them cum.

Chapter Six:
The Calm after the
Storm

Daniel was asleep and Kelly cuddled up to him. Any jealousy she had previously felt about Crystal was gone. Daniel was hers and he was her favorite lover. She smiled and noticed how quiet it had gotten.

Kelly noticed light peeking out from behind the drapes. The sun was coming up and there was no chance of anything else coming up this morning. She looked around. All five men were sexually exhausted and at least three of them were asleep. She was finished too. She was sexually satisfied... well, for now.

She smiled as she drifted off to sleep. Hours later, she woke to the sounds of the shower. She was still cuddled up with Daniel and they had a blanket over them. The shower seemed to be continuous as people showered, dressed and left until only Daniel and her were left. Some people left money for the room and as she counted it, it more than covered the room.

She let Daniel sleep and went to take a shower.

This has been quite the adventure, she thought as she let the water fall onto her body. From one night stands, meeting Daniel, sharing lovers with him and now orgies with ten people. What could possibly be next?

She knew the answer to that question. Next month's meeting of the Orgy Club, that's what. The same people hopefully, but everything will be different. She looked forward to losing herself in lust again with these people.

Daniel opened the shower door and it surprised her. "Good morning," he said. His voice reflected that he was still half asleep.

She looked down and his cock was fully awake.

"Really?" She said. "Doesn't that thing ever get enough?"

"Not with you around."

After cleaning it with soap and rinsing it off, she dropped to her knees. "Okay let's see how much cum you have left. I bet you that it isn't much."

As Kelly gladly sucked on her husband's dick she started to plan next month's meeting. She was happy that they had started this club and she enthusiastically transferred that happiness to the blow job that she was giving.

"You are the best!" He said.

And don't you forget that, she thought.

About the Author

Rachel Richards is an oversexed redhead who loves adult playtime and spends her time writing and doing "research" for her erotic novels. Her novels Kindle are:

`*Swinger Sex Games*': a couple invents ways of seducing other couples.

`*Kelly's Wild Side*': Prelude to `*Into the Swing*'. This is the story of how Kelly and Daniel got together.

`*Into the Swing*': after a number of false starts, Kelly and Daniel enter into the swinging lifestyle.

`*Full Swing*': Kelly and Daniel go deeper into the lifestyle and attend their first orgy.

`*50 Shades of Gay*': an older woman seduces a beautiful young woman into the lesbian world.

`*More 50 Shades of Gay*': a young beautiful woman experiments with both men and women to determine which sex she prefers.

`*The Promiscuous Games*': a parody of the Hunger Games where people compete to see who can out sex the other. Only the winner can continue having sex.

`*Confessions of a Gym Teacher*': Beth Porter is a

gym teacher who is tricked into sleeping with some of her older students. Note: all characters are over 18 years of age.

All titles are available as eBooks by Blue Ops on Kindle. The following are Blue Ops Titles by Rachel that are available on all eBook formats:

`Into the Swing'

`Swinger Sex Games'

`Slut Wife'

The following are titles by Blue Ops author Dick Talent:

`Swinging Vacation'

`I Married a Nympho'

Some of the above titles will be coming to paper-back soon.

www.ingramcontent.com/pod-product-compliance
Lightning Source LLC
Chambersburg PA
CBHW071956170626
46813CB00005B/1900